COOPER

king of cushion island

montse ganges
emilio urberuaga

Published in 2009 by Windmill Books, LLC
303 Park Avenue South, Suite # 1280, New York, NY 10010-3657

                        Publisher Cataloging Data
Ganges, Montse
        Cooper, king of Cushion Island / M. Ganges and E. Urberuaga.
                p. cm. – (Cooper)
        Summary: Although Cooper takes naps on the rug, the armchair, and the sunny
balcony during the day, he always sleeps on his dog bed at night, where he has both good and bad dreams.
        ISBN 978-1-60754-242-1 – ISBN 978-1-60754-243-8 (pbk.)
ISBN 978-1-60754-244-5 (6-pack)
        1. Dogs—Juvenile fiction   2. Dreams—Juvenile fiction   [I. Dogs—Fiction   2. Dreams—Fiction]   I. Urberuaga, Emilio   II. Title
III. Series
        [E]—dc22

Printed in the United States of America

For more great fiction and nonfiction, go to www.windmillbooks.com.

alphabet
soup
an imprint of
WINDMILL
BOOKS
New York

Cooper spends the day taking
little naps. On the thick rug,
in the fluffy armchair,
on the sunny balcony,
on the cool bathroom floor,
next to the laundry basket…
But at night,
Cooper always goes to
sleep on his cushion.

If he's having a good dream,
Cooper sleeps with his paws in the air,
as if he is falling from the sky.
If he's having a nightmare,
Cooper snarls, howls, and doubles
over, as if he has a stomachache.

One of Cooper's best dreams
is that he puts on a cape and
turns into Supersmeller,
the superhero with the most
sensitive nose in the world!
Supersmeller finds everything
people have lost:
socks, friends, puppies…
and people thank him and
present him with a medal.

One of Cooper's nightmares is that everyone goes on vacation and leaves him behind. He's alone in the house and very afraid, and suddenly the Dust Mop Monster comes to chase him!

Another good dream Cooper
has is that he is a great inventor.
He invents a toilet for dogs so
he does not have to do his
business in front of everyone
or go outside in the rain to do it.

A bad dream Cooper has is
that the vet puts one of those
plastic shields around his head,
and it is so big that his head
looks like one little piece of popcorn
at the bottom of a giant bag.

12

A good dream for Cooper is that
he's the goalie of a soccer team
and he blocks a goal to win the game.
The whole stadium chants his name and
the other players hoist him into the air
and carry him around on their shoulders.

A bad dream is that a Terrifying Mole
finds the hiding place where
Cooper buries his treasures.
The mole nibbles Cooper's biscuits
and steals his toy that goes "SQUEAK!"

A good dream is that the mail
carrier brings him a package.
He opens it and finds
The Box of Food
That Is Never Empty,
with a note that says,
"So you'll never be hungry.
Love and kisses,
Mom."

A bad dream is that it's getting late and he's sleepy but he can't find his cushion. He looks everywhere for it, but the cushion has gone without even saying goodbye.

20

A good dream is that he's
the captain of *The Terrier*,
the most fearsome ship on the seas.
Every night the ship
lands on Cushion Island,
because there it is safe
and nothing bad can happen.

Cooper sleeps with his paws in the air and
dreams that he's King of Cushion Island,
ruler of all dreams,
the good ones and the bad

24